Bridget Wants To Play

by
Dearbháil Lynch

Illustrated by Anthony Corrigan

First published 2022
by Triangle House Publishing

Illustrated by Anthony Corrigan

ISBN: 978-1-3999-3768-9

For Cora and Eoin

It takes some people time to get used to their skin,
while others shed the old to show the new within.

Bridget, the caterpillar, was bored one day, so she decided she'd ask some friends to play.

She went into the garden where she met
Goretti, the glow-worm. Goretti was busy
doing her stretches. She was glowing.

'Would you like to play?'
asked Bridget.

'I'd love to have fun and I'd love to play, but I'm practising my glowing today,' said Goretti. 'Can you glow, Bridget?'

Bridget looked at her bottom and tried to make it glow, but she couldn't.

She shrugged. Practising glowing would be boring, she thought, so she went off to the pond.

At the pond, Bridget met Fergal and Fiona, the frogs. Fergal and Fiona were hopping around.

'Would you like to play?' asked Bridget.

'We'd love to have fun and we'd love to play, but we're practising our hopping today,' said Fiona. 'Can you hop, Bridget?'

Bridget tried to hop, but she couldn't.

She shrugged. Practising hopping would be
really boring, she thought, so she went off
to the park.

At the park,
Bridget met Brian,
the bumblebee.
Brian was buzzing.

'Would you like
to play?' asked
Bridget.

'I'd love to have fun and I'd love to play, but I'm practising my buzzing sounds today,' said Brian. 'Can you buzz, Bridget?'

Bridget tried to make a buzzing sound,
but she couldn't.

She shrugged. Practising buzzing
would be very, very boring,
she thought, so she returned home,
a little sad that no one
wanted to play.

'Everyone's too busy to play,' Bridget said to her mother with a big sigh, 'and there's nothing for me to do.'

'You'll find something that you love to do,' said her mother. 'Be patient and see what's meant just for you.'

Bridget closed her eyes, hoping she'd see exactly what that something could be, and fell into a long, deep sleep.

When she woke up she was startled to see two bright yellow wings attached to her body.

Bridget rushed
downstairs to ask
her mother what
she should do.

'Why don't you practise flying, Bridget?'
her mother said.

Bridget wasn't sure
if she'd like to fly.
She'd certainly
never practised
flying.

But she went outside
and climbed to the top
of the high wall.

Then she counted one,
two, three, and jumped
off the wall just to see.

Well, Bridget soared out over the garden where Goretti, the glow-worm, was still glowing ...

... over the pond, where Fergal and Fiona, the frogs, were still hopping ...

... and over the park where Brian, the bumblebee, was still buzzing.

Bridget's friends were very impressed
to see her fly, and Bridget was glad
to have found something
she could do at last.

Flying was fun and Bridget decided to practise her flying.

Practising flying was not at all boring and so she practised every single day.

Except on Saturdays.
On Saturdays, Bridget wanted to play,
and so did all of her friends.

The End

Actually, that was just the beginning...

Dearbháil Lynch worked as an actor and teacher before beginning a career in psychology. She lives in Newry, Co. Down, with her husband, two children and a very fluffy dog called Coco.

Her first book, *Bridget Wants To Play*, is a tale of self-discovery, showing that not everyone is meant to keep their feet on the ground.

Anthony Corrigan is an animator and illustrator. He lives in Newry, Co. Down.

Printed in Great Britain
by Amazon

18732869R00025